"The cold is ever pr
Child of Hameln; it s
you wind your way t
you know. Turner ha
refashioned it for a r
exploring the fear th
donment, isolation a
a small town tragedy. Turner doesn't shy away
from blood and gore, nor from the dark allure
of what's waiting in the woods. Wrap up
against the winter weather and hunker down
with this chilling novella."
— Kathryn Blair, author of *Jesus Loves You God
Hasn't Decided Yet*

"Rarely have I enjoyed a retelling so much;
Child of Hameln subverts expectations and
takes a totally new angle to a familiar murine
tale. Turner's ability to draw the reader fully into
the bitter cold of the small town of Elk Pass —
made even colder and more bitter by its dark,
mysterious history — will have you retreating
under the thickest blanket you can find. Fans of
Twin Peaks will delight in this atmospheric,
vengeful story."
— Lindz McLeod, author of *Beast* and
Turducken

Thank you!

A special thank you from the Knight Errant team to our supporters who backed our 2023 list campaign and made this another exciting year in books for our team and writers.

In no particular order we would like to thank our Generous Benefactor backers Argonaut Books, Caith, Frederick Rossero, Barry Norton, Sam Hirst and Charles Page for their support.

We would also like to thank Ian W. and Jamie Graham for their unprecedented generosity and support for the small arts. Thank you all! You, our readers, make these projects possible.

Published by Knight Errant Press CIC
Falkirk, Scotland
www.knighterrantpress.com

Cover art copyright © Ares Bor, 2023

Design and typesetting by Nathaniel Kunitsky

ISBN (paperback): 978-1-9996713-9-6
eISBN (ebook): 978-1-916665-02-6

Printed and bound in Great Britain by Clays Ltd, Elcograf S.p.A

Knight Errant Press acknowledges support for this title from a Kickstarter campaign, which was partially funded by the Creative Scotland Forward Funds programme.

THE CHILD OF HAMELN

by

Max Turner

Knight Errant Press

2023

CONTENT WARNING

In order of severity and frequency: death, homicide, mentions of cannibalism, graphic gore, loss of a loved one, child neglect, kidnapping, manipulation, mentions of alcoholism, mentions of cancer, threat of isolation, homophobia.

THE CHILD OF HAMELN

BY

MAX TURNER

Chapter One

1961

"Show yourself." Sheriff Williams' voice strained with frustration and anger as he held his gun and torch together, pointing at the treeline. The snow had fallen heavily the day before and there were no fresh tracks that he could see, but there was definitely something at the edge of the woods. When he'd taken the call, he had expected it to be nothing, just someone's overactive imagination.

But there was *something*.

James Williams didn't want to be out on a night like this. With the first snow falling there was already enough to do. A few more days of snowfall at this rate and their town will be cut off for winter a little earlier than usual. This year the mayor had proposed some measures to keep the high road and bridge out of town clear, but they still needed to prepare for their potential and usual isolation if it didn't work.

With that, the Reitz situation and the recent infestation of rodents overrunning the town, Williams had better shit to do than chasing down what was likely a bobcat at most.

The shrubbery rustled and he cocked his gun. Then he heard a pitiful voice, barely more than a quiet sob.

"Sheriff?"

Through fog that fell heavily about the town no matter the time of year, Williams saw a small boy stagger from the edge of the woods. He was dressed in pyjamas, torn by the rough foliage: his skin pale, eyes rimmed so red and raw that it was visible even in the growing darkness of the early winter evening. His bare feet were muddy and covered in cuts and bruises.

Williams hesitated a moment before he uncocked and holstered his gun and started forward, picking up speed as he saw the child start to stumble. He caught him and cradled the limp and exhausted form as the child struggled to regulate his breathing. His eyes were wide with terror and sadness.

"Bobby? Bobby Taylor?" Williams recognised the sickly little kid as that of Bill Taylor, a local drunk. A quiet kid from what he knew, kept to himself. He always went to and from school on his own, smaller than most kids his age and a bit of a loner. He was the kind of kid that Williams always kept an eye on.

He'll probably just become a drunk like his old man, was what most people thought, no one expected Bobby to do better than the family he came from. But he wasn't trouble, he was quiet and polite to a fault. The kind of politeness that was beaten into a kid.

He was the last person James had expected to

see out here, alone at the edge of the woods while he was responding to reports of strange noises that seemed to have the nearest residents terrified.

"The others," Bobby mumbled quietly, shaking in his arms despite feeling burning hot. The kid seemed sick, maybe from walking in the woods at night in barely a stitch. "I can't feel them anymore… The music's gone…"

"Others?"

"The children… the oth–other children," Bobby's breath stuttered against a sob. "They're gone. I couldn't keep up. He left me behind. He took the music away."

The tears came. Williams got to his feet, holding the boy to his chest he carried him back to his vehicle. He had no clue what the hell was going on. His first thought had been that little Bobby had gotten into his daddy's liquor, but he didn't smell of alcohol.

Maybe he was sickening for something, delirious?

The low light of the headlamps and the static, coloured light on the roof lit the way as Williams walked towards his truck, frantic chatter on the radio becoming apparent. He frowned, making out the voice of the dispatcher as he got closer, feeling his pulse spike as he heard the panic in the urgency of her tone.

"Sheriff, please come in. Sheriff!" She was

pleading over and over. Williams picked up the pace, opened the door awkwardly and slid Bobby gently into the passenger seat before grabbing the CB. The wire strained as he pressed the receiver.

"This is Williams."

"Sheriff, oh God, please, you've gotta get back here."

"Okay, okay, slow down. What's going on?" He looked down at Bobby who had curled into a ball, looking like the smallest ten-year-old in the world at that moment.

"James, the children. They're all gone." The words broke on a sob.

"What children?" James growled, frustrated and confused and not getting answers damn well fast enough.

"All of them. All the children from the town. They're all gone, James. Oh God, they're all gone... The calls, the parents are... the phone is ringing off the hook. Someone has taken all the children."

The words trailed off into more sobs and Williams felt a shiver so cold grip him that he couldn't help the uncharacteristic shudder that took hold of his body. He looked down at Bobby who curled in even tighter around his middle as he let out a chilling sob.

1981

Bobby rubbed the bridge of his nose as he walked through the cabin, his feet chilled by the bare wooden floor. He made his way to the kitchen; he'd have enough time to grab a coffee before he packed Buck into the back of his duty truck and clocked in for the day.

One of the floorboards creaked loudly as he walked the hallway.

Damn loud and getting louder every day. He'd not done much with the place since his dad died. Seemed a little pointless.

Though it wasn't really, of course, if he planned on keeping it. Which seemed ever more likely.

He just *wanted* it to be pointless, he wanted to move out. He wanted to sell the place or knock it down. He'd never wanted to come back here after he had moved into his little apartment over the store on the High Street, so many years ago now it felt like a dream more than a memory. But when his dad got sick, the old bastard had no one. No one but Bobby to come back and nurse the miserable asshole as he died slowly, his liver repaying the damage done over the years.

And Bobby had stayed. Letting his apartment go after a few months, becoming stuck in this dank place full of death.

He remembered pulling off all the curtains

the day they took his dad to the funeral home, throwing out the half-rotted old material that had been up since his mum had left decades earlier. He'd replaced them all now, but for weeks he'd just let the sun into this dark and dead place.

He got Buck in part to bring some life to it and to snub his nose at the ghost of his dad. He would never let Bobby have a dog; he'd seen them as a needless expense when that money could be spent on booze. He was likely rolling in his grave and Bobby didn't remotely give a shit.

It had been a damn lonely childhood with no friends. He'd had few enough before the entire town's population under the age of twelve went missing that cold winter's night. After that, the few that remained were older, and all considered him with suspicion given what they knew of that night. That Bobby was the only one not taken.

So many families moved away after that.

They'd closed the school eventually, leaving Bobby and the handful of remaining teens having to attend schools in the next town. Having a dog for companionship might have been nice back then.

As it was, he'd just kept to himself even more than before. No longer just the son of the local drunk, but also the kid — the one. *That one.*

That one that got away, as the townsfolk saw

it, when more deserving children didn't.

Why him? He could see the question and the anger in the faces of the adults who no longer had children. It was almost like some of them blamed him, or at least hated him for something beyond his control — for being the one left behind instead of their child or children.

Why him? Why wasn't one of their kids saved? Why did the quiet little weird kid whose mom walked out and whose dad drank himself into oblivion every night have to come back and not their precious straight-A kid?

Bobby never had to ask himself that because he knew the answer.

When the music had started, he had tried to follow it, as they all had. He'd tried to keep up with the other kids, but his dad had been drunk a solid month and Bobby was malnourished — eking out the random canned goods in the cupboard.

He couldn't keep up because he just didn't have the strength. He wondered if that might have been the time he would have finally died of neglect had the other children not been taken.

Would he have just died in the woods if the Sheriff hadn't taken him to the small community hospital? They had kept him there for two weeks to check him over, feed him up and start getting him well again.

As soon as he was old enough, he'd got his

own place. Just a rented room at first. It was only once James took him under his wing and started mentoring him in the Sheriff's department that people even gave him the time of day. For over a decade now he'd been a well-respected member of the community, like people had forgotten the kid he had been and what he represented to them.

A disassociation to make life easier, Bobby could see right through it.

Almost like the town had collectively agreed to suppress anything too upsetting. His mum had always told him he had a special gift for understanding people and spun him tales of her great-grandmother being a fortune teller. Those tantalising stories were some of the things that had stuck with him, while elsewhere she had left huge holes in his memory. Maybe there was some truth in them, because it seemed like he could always feel the sadness these people were hiding, no matter how hard they tried to conceal it.

Despite his association with the Sheriff, Bobby wasn't fully accepted until he had proved his worth to the town.

Derek Robson's kid Cindy was one of the children that went missing. Derek was one of the many parents, who, over the years, continued to struggle and were unable to deal with their loss and grief. When his wife said she was leaving, he lost the last shred of reason that held him together.

Bobby had been on the job less than six months when he responded to the call out, the closest one to the scene. When Robson ran screaming after his wife with his shotgun at the ready, Bobby pulled the trigger as soon as he saw Robson's finger start to squeeze. Robson's shot went wide of the target, while Bobby's whistled cleanly through the man's neck, jugular and all.

Bobby was shaken up. It had been unexpected, and he had never really considered before that he might sometimes have to kill in the line of duty. But moreover, he was shaken by the feeling it gave him. Something raw and powerful that he didn't dare to dissect.

Not pleasure, not that. But a sense of control he had never felt before and didn't dare look at too closely, in case he found himself wanting more of it.

After the incident, James rallied around him, gave him the support he needed after having to put down a perp. He had been there for Bobby and then so had the town. After years of the Sheriff saying Bobby was a good kid and worth people's time, they started to agree.

It felt like there had been a collective sigh of

relief once he began to integrate into the community at the cusp of his twenties. It felt like they had all been longing for a day when he would either leave or else do something that would mark him out. Now he was the young deputy who saved Mrs Robson. No longer was he *that kid*, and the relief was palpable.

Bobby sighed as he poured out the remnants of yesterday's coffee and started over.

On the surface it might have seemed that the town of Elk Pass was finally healing from their communal tragedy. But the truth of it was that it was easier for them to pretend everything was fine.

Just damn fine.

Bobby could see the truth of it.

As the coffee percolated, he sat down to pull on his socks and boots, once again considering that demolishing this old house and moving into the town proper wasn't going to solve a damn thing.

Too many ghosts lurking about the place, one way or the other.

Bobby grunted as he got to his feet, putting on his holster, sidearm and his old hunting knife. He grabbed his coffee and whistled for Buck, locking up as the dog jumped up into the flat bed, ready for the day ahead.

"Getting cold out there." Bobby said, clapping his fur lined gloves together as he got into the Sheriff's office. When he received no response he pulled them off and threw them onto James' desk. Snow was in the air, even more oppressive than the perpetual fog.

"Hey!" James protested. Bobby frowned a little.

He knew that tone wasn't one of annoyance; James hadn't heard him come in. Bobby put the thought aside, he didn't want to admit that James was getting old just as much as the Sheriff himself didn't.

The outer office was bustling with everyone checking in or checking out. Bryony Zimmerman had just poured herself a cup of strong coffee and settled in at the dispatcher's desk, not removing her scarf. She gave Bobby that half-wary smile of hers as Buck trotted into the inner office. A few years older than him, she'd been one of the teens spared. Too old to be taken that night.

Bobby watched as Buck went to the noisy little heater next to James' desk and slumped down in front of it. He shared a look with Bryony, both pointedly ignoring James collecting himself as he drew back from the paperwork; courteously ignoring the eccentricities that were increasing month by month.

James wasn't as focused anymore; he was well past retirement, but Bobby knew he felt some intrinsic responsibility for the town. Bobby understood it, even if he did worry about James' health. There was a strange energy about this town that even Bobby felt, despite having lived nowhere else and having no basis for comparison. He knew other towns didn't feel like this.

James seemed to think it was his duty to keep *it* in check. Whatever *it* was, intangible and dark.

It felt almost oppressive over the last week.

It didn't help that the snow was coming in. Within the next couple of days they'd be up to their necks in it, the town would be all but engulfed by it.

"Do your patrol James, then go home. Have lunch with Mary. Bring me back a sandwich." Bobby grinned, slapping his mentor on the back even as the older man grumbled. Bobby continued, "I've got everything under control. Already checked the road and we're fine. Even if the snow arrives tonight, we're fine. The road will be open."

He knew it was a source of anxiety for the man. Hell, not just for James, for the whole town. Keeping the town open even when the snow threatened to cut them off from the world, as it once had been able to do, was a necessity if people were going to sleep at night.

"The drift blocks are up and all the ploughs are ready to go," Bobby said softly, a hand on James' shoulder. "They're parked just off the road. Just waiting for old man Price to start scattering the salt on the bridge and high road. It's under control."

James finally nodded and stood up, moving slowly in the cold office as he grabbed his coat. Worry was etched in his face, and Bobby knew it would remain there until the thaw in spring. But even so, there seemed to be something more to it this year. Maybe James was under the weather? He'd seemed off the last week or so, declining faster, though towards what Bobby wasn't sure.

Retirement, he hoped.

It couldn't just be the stress about the high road. The road and bridge out of town had only ever been impassable a handful of winters since Bobby was a kid. Sometimes their measures didn't work out and the town was cut off for the whole of the winter. Sometimes the snow came in too fast and too heavy, and stuck the ploughs. Sometimes it rained at the wrong time, and it was the ice that became impassable. And if they couldn't act fast on the worse than usual conditions, then it became too bad to resolve. One year the ploughs themselves ended up completely buried in a snowdrift that they couldn't dig out for weeks, until conditions eased.

Bobby remembered those times well, especially the most recent one during his third year as a Deputy. The whole town had held its collective breath in fear of being isolated again. That was when they felt it the most, the strangeness of Elk Pass. The heavy feeling that Bobby wanted to call evil.

As James let himself out, the crisp coolness of the air — how still it was before the snow — caught Bobby's breath as it filled the room for a moment. In winter it felt like the whole town waited for death, and Bobby knew that better than anyone.

It was going to be a long day, and he knew two things were certain: lunch would be one of Mary's chicken salad sandwiches and he wouldn't sleep well tonight.

✕━━✕

The beast loomed over him. So close he could almost reach out and touch him.

His breath fogged the air above Bobby's bed as he lay there frozen.

*He wanted to move. He **wanted** to reach out. He wanted to touch —*

"You're mine, Bobby Taylor. I will come for you one day." The words were lyrical, musical. The same

sound that he had heard as a child, the sound he had wanted to follow. The beast leaned over him, Bobby could feel his icy cold breath against the side of his face. "Remember you are mine."

"Never fear what you might become, sweetheart."

Bobby woke with a start at the sound of his mother's voice, and the words she had spoken to him often. His body trembled, dripping with sweat, he panted and his breath froze in the air. He was an uncomfortable mixture of hot and cold as the sweat rolled down his skin. He tried to calm himself, sucking in breaths that did nothing to steady him.

He let out a sob, unable to hold it back. Just the one sharp noise that echoed around him in the empty room.

He scrubbed his hands roughly over his face, running them up through his damp hair as he let out a heavy breath. Every damn winter he was plagued by these dreams.

Nightmares.

The music.

The terrible and entrancing sound that drew them all from their homes that night.

The figure — no, a shadow — blacker than the night with a crown of thicket and brambles, and talons for fingers. Bobby had known he should have been afraid, but he wasn't. He knew the appearance of the beast should have horrified him. He knew he should have found it terrifying. Instead he found it beautiful.

He *was* beautiful. And Bobby had wanted to follow him.

He'd wanted to follow so desperately.

Every winter he had these dreams and woke with the terror of regret. The knowledge that he should have been taken too. The heavy knowledge that he should feel relief, that he should be thankful to have been left behind.

But when he remembered how it had felt that night, he didn't feel that way at all.

Most of the time he tried to feel little, one way or the other, about it; ignore it and try to leave it in the past. But during the winter months, he felt raw and these dreams always came like clockwork.

Nightmares that should remind him of how lucky he was to have escaped.

But they weren't nightmares because of what he had escaped, but because of what he had missed. He trembled with fear because of the loss he had suffered, the memory of it cutting him deep, over and over.

He would end up replaying that night in a strange haze.

Falling behind. Coughing and sick, unable to catch up. Weak and worthless. The music started to fade, the children and the beast that led them became distant, obscured by the snow that didn't feel cold until the sheriff found him.

Bobby wrapped the blankets around his shoulders and stood, moving to the window and looking out. The snow was already falling.

Remember you are mine.

Bobby shivered.

He wasn't. He wasn't anybody's.

He was alone and abandoned.

"Bobby?" The voice down the phone pitched high on a sob, but Bobby knew it well enough.

Mary Williams.

She has been as good as family to him since he'd left the hospital twenty years ago, her and James had pulled the slack left by his father. They'd given him a home from home, cooked meals and a pull-out to sleep on when his dad was too drunk to remember he even had a kid.

"Mary? What is it?" He put down his coffee, feeling a cold shiver travel down his spine.

The obvious concern in his voice brought a low whimper from Buck, who drew up next to his kitchen stool and leaned into his leg. It was a little before nine, though the clouds were so dense it looked like it could still be the middle of the night.

The hour of sleep Bobby managed before the

nightmare had made him drowsy. Now he was wide awake.

"It's James. He... Bobby, he's gone."

He knew immediately what she meant. He knew it with a certainty that resonated deeply through his core, leaving a pressure in his chest. He wondered if this was the telepathy his mother had talked of when he was little. He could feel Mary's unspoken pain and loss as his own, even her underlying concern over having to tell him. Her concern for how *he* would feel. A sense of her loss was filled with the pain of his own.

"I'm coming over."

By the time Bobby pulled up outside the Williams' house, a couple of neighbours were gathered on the porch and the coroner's van was pulling away, driving slowly from the house in the increasingly heavier snowfall.

Bobby jumped out of the truck, Buck on his heels as he ran up the stoop and let himself in as he always had.

"Mary?"

He saw her straight away. She stood looking out the window, with a tissue held to her face, but otherwise composed with her usual quiet dignity, watching the coroner's car pull away and disappear into the flurry of snow. She turned to him and gave him a comforting smile, and it broke Bobby's heart that her first instinct was to comfort him rather than seek any for herself.

He went over to her and rested a hand lightly on her arm. She smiled.

"They think it was a heart attack. I was up early, let him sleep in. When he hadn't come down after a while, I went up to check and he… they think he went peacefully. Might not have even woken up. You know, he thinks… he thought of you as a son. We could never have any of our own and… the night that monster took all the children but left you, you were a blessing to us, Bobby."

She took his hands in hers and a tear rolled quietly down her cheek. Bobby felt a tight pain in his throat that had been absent at the death of his own father.

He sat and comforted her a while, though she put on a brave face and told Bobby not to worry. Her friends rallied around and were sweet to him, making them both sweet tea. One by one they came and went, until only Mrs Hodson remained and insisted on making Mary some lunch.

She was busying herself in the kitchen when Mary turned to Bobby, her brows knitting into a deep frown of concern, one he hadn't seen since the days when he'd turn up at their door with a black eye or a bruised wrist courtesy of his dad.

"Bobby, there are a lot of things over the years

that James only half told me, to save my feelings. And I accepted that, that's what it is to be married to someone in law enforcement. But there was always something he wanted to say, to tell me. And I think... I think he wanted to tell you, too. I think that's what this is." She pulled an envelope from her pocket and handed it to him.

Bobby took the letter, recognising his name in James' handwriting, he looked at it a moment before sliding it into his own pocket at the little noise from the kitchen. It was private. He knew he would likely eventually share it with Mary, whatever it was, but not now. Not here.

Mary's expression was still burdened as she seemed to fight an internal battle before saying anything further.

"Did James tell you about Frederick Reitz?"

The name rang the faintest of bells and Bobby cocked his head, "I don't think I've met him."

Mary shook her head. "No, no you wouldn't have. He's... his family used to live here; he's been back in town this last week. The old house, the big one out by the woods."

Bobby frowned. "He's living there? It's abandoned, I don't think it even has electricity connected."

Mary played with the hem of her sleeve, a nervous habit.

"The Reitz House," Mary muttered then shook her head. "I don't know, he's probably at the hotel or the guest house, James didn't say."

That was where the bell had rung, Bobby realised. People had called it that when he was a kid, but these days it was just known as the 'Firebug Place'. It was just off of Firebug Lane, so named because of the propensity of the insects there every year, despite the town not even remotely having the ideal conditions for the species to thrive.

He was sure no one had called it the 'Reitz House' in years. It was damn near derelict — they included it in a patrol now and then along with some other outlying or disused properties about the town.

"You should maybe check on him? Let him know about James? I think his visit was in part to see James but... I can't explain all that. I don't know it all. I know James thought he owed the man something."

She ran out of words and Bobby could feel that she was considering James. That he had always felt responsible for too many people, the whole town really.

He squeezed her hands and smiled.

"I'll take care of it, Mary. Don't worry."

By the time he left Mary at the house with Mrs Hodson and their lunch, he was emotionally drained. It was hard to imagine the town — that life in general — could continue without the imposing personality of James Williams. Looming over all of them like a father, a kindly patriarch who kept them all safe.

Bobby swapped his shift with another deputy and went home.

It was evening before he addressed the letter he'd been considering all day. He settled with a glass of whiskey, took it out of his coat pocket and opened it briskly.

Bobby,

If you're reading this then I'm gone, and maybe that isn't a surprise. I've not been well, I've been getting old, and nothing gets past you.

I expect you're thinking that this is a letter asking you to take care of Mary for me. But you know as well as anyone, that woman needs no one to take care of her and she'd cuss me out for suggesting it.

If you're reading this then I never had the balls to tell you something I should have told you long ago. I always told myself I would explain when you were older, and that day never seemed to come. I guess I'm a coward.

I never really told you what happened that night I found you in the woods. I know your memory is sketchy — simplified. The memory of a child who knew no more than his immediate facts. And a child that had just been through a trauma, at that.

There was more to it than what you remember.

I know you pieced together some of it yourself over the years. You know about the infestation, all the rats. But I don't think you ever knew the whole story.

I never told you about Frederick Reitz.

Bobby, if I'm honest I'd like to go to my grave knowing that you'd never know more than you already do, but I don't have that luxury. I've lived in fear all these years, of history repeating itself. Without me there, it falls to you. There is an evil in this town, and I've tried for decades to contain it anyway I could, anyway I was able, and it's never really been enough.

The files are all in my office, you'll find them in my cabinet. Look under Reitz. It's all there. And I'm sorry Bobby. I'm sorry for my part in all of this and having to

leave it all with you. You deserve better.
You're a good kid. A fine man. A better
person than most in this town.

And please take care of Mary all the
same.

James

Bobby set down his glass and sighed out a quiet sob. The reality of James' death seemed to loom over him, and he had no idea how to process it.

With his own father he had waited and prayed for death as the man slowly wasted in his own spite and bile. This was sudden and painful. A sharp and searing pain cutting through him that was only dulled slightly by the intrigue left in the man's wake.

Bobby took a few deep breaths and buried a hand in Buck's coat where he sat beside him — allowed himself a few quiet tears.

Then he wiped his face, grabbed his coat and keys to the sheriff's office.

Chapter Two

"Succulent," there was a laugh and a lip-smacking noise, interlaced with the crackling and background sounds of an old and worn cassette tape.

The word echoed off the cold walls of the empty inner office. The warmth and spirit of the place seemed to have died along with James.

There had been a subdued and polite nod when Bobby had arrived to find the door closed and the night duty Deputy using a free desk in the outer office. The whole place was almost silent despite the Deputy and the night duty dispatcher sitting close enough for chatter.

Bobby had turned the heating on when he arrived, but the little electric space heater seemed no competition for the coming winter. When Bobby had left Mary, the snow was getting heavy, heavier still when he left his own home, but now it was coming down so thick that visibility was almost non-existent. It seemed much heavier and faster than usual.

Bobby had a dire thought that they would be cut off by the morning at this rate. He made a mental note to check that the salt and ploughs were sorted as they should have been. It could be a total whiteout soon and he wondered if he should just grab the file and go home, get snowed in there rather than the terribly empty-feeling office.

But when he busted open James' filing cabinet, what he found kept him there.

He wasn't sure what he'd been expecting. Not this? Or maybe he had.

The file was thick, everything from official reports to news clippings. When Bobby had lifted it onto the desk, the cassette tape had come loose and fallen out. The label read: *Allen, R. Interview November 1st, 1951*

Bobby grabbed the cassette player from his own desk drawer and set it out, popping in the tape as he started to flick through the file.

When Allen, R. started to laugh Bobby stopped the tape and wound it back to the beginning so that he could get the context. What did this tape have to do with anything?

It wasn't initially clear from the file, which so far was a wad of news clippings about the disappearance of the children. Some even mentioned him. And he knew as much as anyone on that subject, surely?

As the tape strained to a stop and then clicked off, Bobby pressed play.

Allen. That was the name of the old mayor, the one from when he was a kid. The Allens were one of those rich families that had made money in timber or livestock and built themselves a nice property on the edge of the town.

Didn't hear talk of them much nowadays, but Bobby was sure they had run the local meat industry, that was the root of their wealth, generations of it. They were the subject of some hushed gossip, but only since the death of the mayor a few years ago.

Bobby had hardly heard of them before that, but then he had become aware of the daughter, Dawn, having inherited everything instead of her older brother, as had been expected.

The more Bobby thought on it the more he recalled, though mostly through idle gossip. Rumours that the mayor's son was possibly institutionalised. Their estate was barely at the edge of the town limits, so it never seemed pertinent to know more and he was not one for gossip. Now Bobby wondered if he should have paid more attention.

"This is Interview…" the recording started to crackle as though the beginning of the tape had been mangled. "…Reitz, and Marlene Reitz…" the voice continued but then the crackle worsened; Bobby wound it on a few seconds forward and played it again. This time the quality was poor, but he could hear the same voice that had said 'succulent'.

It was not a kind voice.

"Oh yes, freely."

"You're willing to sign a confession stating that?" The voice that appeared at the beginning of the tape. Bobby vaguely recognised it as one of the deputies who had retired when he was still a kid.

There was a manic and sickening laughter that went on too long for comfort before Allen spoke again. "Oh yes."

"Randall, are you telling me you are confessing to killing, and eating, the Reitz family?"

"Oh goodness, no. Not eating. Not all of them. You see it was only the girl I wanted but parents do tend to be troublesome in such things. I killed them, and the little one. And then I carved her flesh—"

Bobby's breath stopped, he swallowed, his mouth dry as the words sunk in.

"—it's not so different to butchering a pig, you know. Though she didn't have much meat on her bones." A light and sinister chuckle. "But, what she did have was… succulent." Then came the laugh and the lip-smacking noise, before Allen continued through his laughter, "like a little piggy."

"Fuck," that was clearly muttered by one of the interviewers.

There were some other discrete sounds of discomfort around the room.

Allen continued to laugh like a madman. Bobby felt sick to his stomach, but he had to keep listening, there was something here that James had wanted him to know.

"And what about the boy? Frederick Reitz?"

Bobby's ears perked up at the familiar name as Allen's laughter trailed off.

"Horrid child. Look here, he kicked my shins." There was rustling and the jangle of a cuff. "When I tried to take his sister. I locked him in the cabin… I don't know, some hunting lodge on the estate grounds."

There was commotion and Bobby knew the officers would be passing that information on, getting someone to go looking for the missing boy. For Frederick Reitz.

"And was it the hunting lodge where you obtained the knife, or did you bring that with you?"

"It's my own of course! How else would I test the meat? Father gave it to me, an heirloom. I do hope you return it in good condition when I am released."

Bobby wanted to turn it off. He'd seen some shit as a deputy, it wasn't like there had never been violence in this town. He'd had to deal with Robson, after all, and some people were not well adjusted. But this Allen guy? Was he insane?

It scared Bobby and reassured him at the same time.

When he'd killed Robson, he'd felt… not as he had expected.

He knew killing someone was the worst thing there was. But when it felt just and right? When the someone you killed was attempting to murder their wife?

He hadn't thought twice about emptying a round into the man. And he was always terrified by the fact that he'd do it again. That there was a line in killing someone, and he had found out where his line was. Bobby had not felt remotely bothered by it, only by the fact that he wasn't bothered and what that might say about him.

He had kept hold of the fact that it was attuned to, what he felt, was a good moral compass. And that was now affirmed by this tape.

He knew that not only was he not like Randall Allen and never could be, but that he'd have no problem killing Allen just as he had killed Robson. He surely wouldn't be the first or only officer of the law to have tendencies that one might decide were more akin to vigilantism?

Before Allen could continue there was the sound of commotion and a door opening, people talking heatedly but not close enough to the recorder to be completely clear. Then one gruff voice sounded above the rest, a commanding tone.

"This interview is over. You will not speak to my son again without our lawyer present."

More commotion, then the room was quiet, and Bobby heard a much younger James Williams murmur, "sick fuck." Then static as the recording ended but the tape rolled on, empty.

Bobby startled when the tape finally ended and clicked off.

His palms were sweaty, and Allen's sinister tone echoed around his mind. He realised he was breathing erratically and took a few deep breaths to calm himself before looking back down at the file he had zoned out on.

He removed the top of the pile that was a variety of newspaper clippings over the years, but mostly from the months immediately after the mass disappearance of the town's children. Beneath that were official reports on the disappearance, local and FBI.

Bobby thumbed through them, things he had avoided for years but knew he could have accessed at any time. He wasn't sure he wanted to know what the official reports said, but he flicked through them all the same, one name catching his eye.

Frederick Reitz.

Bobby went back to the top of the section — *Persons of Interest.*

He scanned quickly through the pages. If Reitz was a child when that Allen tape was made, then he couldn't have been one of the kids that went missing. That much was already certain from the fact that Mary had mentioned he was in town visiting. Bobby had kept to himself at school but was sure he knew the names of most of the kids in town and the name Frederick Reitz was unusual enough that he would have surely remembered it, so they must have been years apart.

Frederick Reitz:

Arrived in Elk Pass October 31st, 1961. Last seen by [redacted].

"Redacted?" Bobby frowned and scanned the rest of the page. It was almost unreadable and gave virtually no information, with parts of almost every sentence redacted. He rifled through the rest of the report, it seemed to be the only section given this treatment.

"What the hell?"

Bobby put down the report and carried on through the file. It went from seeming like an archaeological excavation to being one when he unexpectedly hit 1953. He moved everything before that into one pile and picked up the newspaper report.

Case Closed: Reitz Family Slaughter
Remains Unsolved.

Bobby frowned again, looking at the cassette player as though it would give him answers and then back to the headline. This was over a year after the confession he had just heard recorded. How could it have been unsolved if there was a confession right there on tape?

He moved the newspaper clippings and found a notebook; the scrawl on the front told him it belonged to James. When he opened it, he could see the outline and discolouration where the tape he had dropped earlier had clearly been slotted in between a few pages. It had likely been there for years.

Bobby read the first entry. Dated November 1961, a month before the children disappeared.

Mary is sick.

Doctor says it's cancer. It's like this evil force eating her from the inside and I have to ask, is this my fault? Is this punishment?

Bobby stopped reading and swallowed. Mary had told him before about her cancer, she'd been sick when the kids went missing, but by the time James had started to mentor him and take him to their place for dinner, she was recovering. In remission. She'd been cancer free since.

Bobby's hands shook around the book. This was something personal, this was not the notebook of the Sheriff, but of James Williams. It felt intrusive to read it, but James had told him where to find it. He would have known Bobby would read it.

He *wanted* Bobby to read it.

Are we all being punished?

Ten years ago, I listened to a child, a ten-year-old boy, tell me what had happened to his family. His little sister, Marlene. Something I already knew because the sick animal who did it had already given us a confession. And then I had to look that kid in the eyes, tell him I would help him, that I would get him justice, only to have it all go away. To be made a damn liar!

I tried. I tried so hard. But Mary was sick, and I wasn't anybody, just another Deputy.

What could I do?

I should have tried harder.

Bobby flicked through the next few pages. Notes on the Allen case, James' recollections ten years after the fact from the looks of it. Scrawled, with extra notes in some of the margins, like he was trying to get down everything about the case that he knew. And Bobby had to wonder at that.

He put the book aside and carried on through the pile until he found the official investigation report into the murder of the Reitz family. It was quickly clear that there was no mention of Allen. There was nothing about his interview or confession.

Dead end enquiries, no leads.

Bobby let it fall closed and sat back in the chair. What the fuck was going on?

Did the Reitz family murder get covered up?

As if James was answering him, Bobby noticed that something in the piles of paperwork had shifted and was poking out the side of the remaining papers. He pulled at the corner and found a photo.

It looked official, a portrait. A family standing on the steps of the town hall. A man Bobby vaguely recognised as Mayor Allen. With him were two children, a girl no more than three years old who looked sad and distant, and a boy who looked…

If Bobby wanted to describe to someone what evil looked like in a child, he would have shown them this photo. His eyes were dark and menacing.

He shuddered and turned it over. James' handwriting on the back:

Mayor Charles Allen, Randall and Dawn Allen. 1948, Accession.

If Bobby had to guess, the handwriting was angry. The scrawl said as much as the photo itself.

He went back to the report on the murder and started reading again, turning to the profiles of the Reitz family. The Reitz were rich and had influence, some well to do Europeans who had immigrated from a town called Hameln, Germany, in 1933 as the Nazis were rising to power. They were active in the community and well liked. Bobby wondered how he had never really known of them before. Clearly, they were a bloody footnote in the town's history, deemed unworthy of any sort of justice.

Maybe if one of the adults had survived things would have been different. But what was a ten-year-old Frederick Reitz going to do if adults, equally as influential as his parents, wanted to cover something up? As it was, the report stated that some uncle had arrived shortly thereafter and taken young Frederick away with him back to Europe, and that was that.

Case closed and problem solved.

Bobby realised he'd been clenching his jaw as he read.

Anger seethed inside of him. And a sort of pity for James, having lived all these years with the weight of this and any guilt he attributed himself. Bobby could see how it would have been difficult to do something at the time, but in the years since?

He felt drained at the thought of even attempt-ing to drag all this up. But that was exactly what he was going to do, wasn't it? He could only imagine that was James' purpose in telling him about this file. He would have known that Bobby wouldn't have hidden or destroyed it, he would have known Bobby would have acted on this information even if he could never bring himself to.

Where to start was Bobby's first consider-ation.

This was all so convoluted, and in his absorption in the murder of the Reitz family, Bobby realised he had lost sight of the initial concern. That Frederick Reitz, who must have then been twenty years old at the time, had returned to Elk Pass around the time the children went missing. That this information had been reported and then redacted from the case file. That James' focus had been the missing children.

It had always been the children, Bobby remembered.

He had been with James most of that strange night.

When he couldn't keep up, James found him wandering back out of the woods. He had ended up in the Sheriff's car and then the Sheriff's office for some time, the town frantic and James trying to maintain order. It was hours before Bobby was actually taken to the hospital by one of the deputies. And even then there seemed to be this weird reluctance to let him go. No one wanted to lose sight of the one remaining child.

And it didn't end there. Every year on the anniversary of the disappearance James was different. Worked longer hours, patrolled the edge of the woods. Seemed sort of torn between guarding the town against it happening again and waiting for the children to come home.

Bobby went back to James' notebook, flicking through the updates of November 1961. Mostly James felt that he was still unable to do anything about the murder case. One impassioned entry mentioned how he had tried to get a copy of the report before the redactions were applied only to find out that it had been purposefully destroyed.

When he got to mid-December, the entries picked up again. Pages and pages filled in

James' chaotic hand, some of the handwriting smudged in a hurry or a barely readable scrawl. It was the week leading up to the disappearance of the children.

Frederick Reitz visited me today. He remembered me, was polite. Shook my hand. He has something charming about him and I'll admit I was relieved to see how well adjusted he has grown to be.

Who could imagine watching your parents butchered? Losing them and a sister to that monster and his actions.

Imagine returning to a town where that sicko still walks free. I failed that kid, the whole damn town did. Damn the Allens.

There were more of James' thoughts on the Allens, which Bobby skipped over until another entry, a few days later, caught his eye.

The reports of infestations, weird animals, dying vegetation. They seem to be increasing. We're getting more by the day. I don't even know what to tell people — we asked for Fish and Wildlife to send someone out to take a look. They can't get anyone out here before the snow hits and we have no way of knowing if the road will stay open. If we're cut off then we're stuck.

We have been offered help by Frederick Reitz. I'm reticent about it. I don't know that it's right to expect anything from the man at this point. But he says he has a background in wildlife management, he's happy to take a look.

Bobby frowned. He only had vague recollections of the infestations that happened the week leading up to the disappearance. He had never really connected the two in his head before, it was another one of those things that the town had never spoken of. And, of course, it had become overshadowed by the disappearances. He might have thought it hadn't happened at all, but for the fact that his dad caught a rat the size of a cat in a trap on their property.

Bobby skipped over the notes James had made on the progress of the snow clearing, the fact that the snow was predicted to hit much sooner than expected that year. Only briefly taking in the worsening of the situation. Crops failing, livestock dying or being attacked. At this rate they would struggle until spring if the town was cut off by the snow as expected. He could read the panic in James' words, see it in the messy writing.

And then—

Frederick has offered a solution. Says he can come up with a simple but effective method of killing off the infestation. Something to do with noise. Sound. A bunch of stuff I don't understand about sonic frequencies. Music I guess, when it comes down to it.

He just wants one thing in return.

Justice.

This is it. I have to do this now. Ten years is more time than he should have waited. Without his help this town will not survive the winter. We owe it to him and his family to give them justice after all these years.

There were more, shorter and rushed entries detailing the progress being made. Frederick was building some sort of machine that would emit a sound on a frequency that would drive the infestation out. Once the rats got past the town and into open country they would no doubt freeze. James seemed delighted to be working with the young man, even more delighted that Mayor Allen had agreed that if

Frederick succeeded, he would indeed hand his son over to the authorities.

The next entry that Bobby zoned in on was written in heavy ink, as though James had pressed the pen almost through the paper in his rage.

God damn Allen. Damn him to hell!

Frederick did it, as he promised. A clear twenty-four hours now the machine has been running and the town is recovering. He saved the town. This town owes him more than it has any right to and the least he could expect was for the mayor to keep his word.

He laughed. Laughed at me, down the phone when I told him it was time to bring Randall in. Said I was naive to think that it was ever going to happen. He isn't about to give up his son, and what the revelation would do to his reputation, position and business.

Laughed over and over, that the scandal would destroy the town and end many careers, possibly even my own. Talked to me like I was stupid and hadn't already considered that, wasn't already prepared.

I told Frederick, assured him I would do everything within my power. Allen made a liar of me again!

Frederick's gone. He left. Asked to pass onto Allen that whatever happened now was down to him. That anything that befell Elk Pass was on the Allens.

I have truly never been so chilled before

in my life than when he said those words. He was frightening, larger than life. I don't know how he plans to do it, but I'm sure he really does mean to bring this town to justice and maybe that's just fine.

Bobby was shaking as he put down the notebook, wiping sweaty palms on his pant legs. He was becoming invested in this unfolding story, all the more so for it being real. This was something he had never known about James, about the town. This was something that had shaped all their lives, not least his own. For years he had deliberately not sought answers, and now they were being thrust upon him. His chest was tight from the emotion of it. He didn't want to know any of this, much less have the sudden responsibility of unravelling it.

Bobby had never sought these answers because he had never wanted to think about it.

He didn't want to give into that constant urge to spend every waking moment hearing that music and feeling the regret of being left behind. He was meant to have gone with the children, he *wanted* to go with them.

The music still called to him and thrummed in

his blood.

Bobby pulled the book back in front of him and scanned the journal to the next entry.

Did he take the children?

⌖

Bobby shoved the notebook away, struck with the thought of Frederick taking the children. Is that what had happened? He'd always wondered whether his memories were corrupted by the distance from childhood and delirium of malnutrition. Because it hadn't been a man that had taken the children. He had never told James, never told anyone, that it was a beast. The same one that haunted his dreams and exuded beautiful music as though it vibrated off its very skin.

Bobby snapped out of the reverie and riffled through the remaining items in the file, a lot of it was mundane and grounding. Xerox copies of reports of vandalism and such over the years at the edge of the town, the Reitz House. It was clear that James had been keeping an eye on the place.

There were other, slightly strange, reports. Surveys taken annually of the crops and livestock, in the weeks leading up to the anniversary of the disappearance, like he was checking. Bobby's mind went back to the connection James must have started to see between the children, the rodent infestation and Frederick Reitz. He tried to get his mind there, but despite his detective skills there was a disconnect as though this was part reality, part fantasy.

A feeling that was oddly brought home by the final item, tucked at the back of the file, hidden rather than an afterthought. It was a xerox of a children's story, *The Pied Piper of Hameln*.

Bobby had never heard of it. The story was short and to the point, but the pages themselves were annotated with James' writing. Some observations, concerns. A chilling note.

What about Bobby? He shouldn't have been left behind. Will he come back for him some day? I failed Frederick, but maybe I can keep Bobby safe.

At the bottom of the page:

Keep close watch on Randall Allen. Don't let him get away with this again.

Bobby swallowed hard and looked at everything laid out in front of him on the desk. Disorganised now, or so it might seem — little piles of varying sizes and from various times. His thoughts went to James' odd habit on the anniversary of the disappearance. He hadn't noticed at first when he was younger, but had a vague idea as time went on, that on the anniversary of the disappearance James would go on patrol alone regardless of staffing or weather. Bobby only had a clear knowledge of it once he was deputised. He'd even asked Deputy Klein one time who had replied with a shrug that on the anniversary, James would go on his own patrol. Was he patrolling to make sure the infestation hadn't returned? That the children weren't threatened? That Randall Allen didn't hurt anyone again?

This was all just a huge, convoluted mess that somehow made sense in James' mind even if he'd never been able to resolve it.

"This is what you meant, James? This is my responsibility now. Make sure history doesn't repeat itself?"

Right there and then he made the decision to do what James would be doing at this moment. He grabbed the keys to his truck.

Bobby ruffled Buck's fur, the dog now in the passenger seat rather than his usual place in the back. It was dark and cold, snow thick about them, and Buck's breath fogged the air as his tongue lolled out.

Bobby smiled.

"Don't worry buddy, this is only a marginally terrible idea."

Buck whined as Bobby drove through the near impenetrable snow. It was slow going as he headed for the edge of town. He had grabbed the address from the town records, Randall Allen now lived with some older relative, in their apparent care. An old aunt or something. Someone who took care of him at his father's behest rather than him being placed in an institute. Bobby had considered it to be gossip until he had pulled the address information and found notes on the file. She had power of attorney and was listed as his caretaker.

It was on the outskirts, though not as far as the Allens' property. He had to drive past the Reitz House.

Bobby was just passing the end of Firebug Lane, when he noticed lights and movement on the top floor of the not-too-distant house.

"Fuck," he muttered, and Buck whined again. He slowed and made a wide turn to head down the lane towards the abandoned house. "Just a quick detour," he told the dog, patting his head. "Better check out what's going on here." He wondered about stupid kids or cold tramps being stranded out in the dead old house in this weather.

He pulled up outside the house, as close as he could get to the front door, and slid out of the car. The cold punched the air out of him, the wind now bringing the snow in quick and sideways. Ten minutes. He'd give himself ten minutes at most, no matter what he found. He needed to check in on Randall and then... he wasn't sure. He just knew it was what James would do. What would happen once he found the man, he couldn't say.

The short path from the drive was overgrown and obscured by the snow. He picked his way through brambles hidden by the whiteness, to the front of the huge house.

It wasn't technically derelict but portions of it had been boarded up.

Bobby ruminated on how strange it was that he had never much heard the name Reitz before, that he had never known any history of this property. That no one *ever* talked about it, as though it had been abandoned a hundred years ago and faded into the history of the town.

He tried the front door, expecting nothing, surprised when it opened. It was heavy and stiff but didn't take a lot to open it enough to shoulder inside and out of the snow, even as some of it drifted through with him.

Bobby pulled out his torch and turned it on, the steady beam of it catching the dust in the air. He swept it over the foyer, noting the size; the location of the stairs; the furniture covered in sheets. As he took a step forward, into this mausoleum of a house, the torch began to flicker. He tapped it a couple of times, but the beam flickered again and then went out.

"Shit," he muttered, turning it off and on again to no avail.

That was when he heard the click of shoes on once polished wood flooring. The sound echoed for a moment, making it hard to tell its direction at first, and Bobby found his heart starting to race. It didn't sound like the shuffle of a tramp or the scampering of teens. He put one hand on his holster, flicking the catch and ready to draw.

"Hello? Who's there?" He called, the words bouncing off the walls in a way that was more eerie than he would have liked.

A glow of light appeared on the landing of the floor above, leaking through to the top of the stairs and getting brighter as it approached. Bobby felt a strange shiver over his entire body, a vulnerable feeling of being seen when he wanted to hide. The light grew closer and brighter until he could make out it was a lamp, held by a dark figure.

The figure was little more than a black shape. Bobby was blinded by the bright lamp and unable to see clearly. It came to a stop at the top of the stairs and Bobby knew it was looking down on him. He felt like prey and fought the urge to run.

Instead, he was rooted to the spot, trapped by equal parts fear and curiosity. Fear of something overwhelming, a sense of something strange and familiar, not of the figure. The realisation hit him hard, and he swallowed, his mouth dry. Bobby opened it to speak but was cut off before any words had a chance to stumble out.

His radio crackled to life and the dispatcher's concerned tone was clear, even if the signal itself was distorted by the snow.

"Deputy Taylor, please respond. We have… I don't know, reports of vermin. Rats? Bobby there's something going on up near the woods, I'm getting all kinds of crazy reports. Bobby, can you hear me?"

The line crackled a little more, but Bobby found himself watching that unmoving lamp, stock still despite wanting to move. "I've got all kinds of reports about giant rats, they're coming out of the snow, hundreds of them. People are starting to panic. Bobby? Bobby?"

The figure started towards him.

Chapter Three

"Oh god, Bobby—" the line fizzled and Bryony's pitiful words disappeared into snowy static. Bobby was painfully reminded of a similar call twenty years earlier that had come through James' radio.

He shuddered.

"Where are my manners?" The voice was smooth and warm, the tone charming.

The figure started to come into focus as he moved closer, the lamp less blinding as the distance closed. A neatly dressed man, with a concerned smile that sent a strange shiver through him that wasn't entirely unpleasant.

"Bobby, is it?"

"Deputy Taylor," Bobby corrected, his voice breaking around the words. He cleared his throat, trying to ignore the immense power and pull he felt at the closeness of the stranger.

"My apologies. My name is Rick Reitz, Frederick, but Rick always feels less formal." He smiled as though they were making pleasant conversation at a cocktail party. "I arrived last week and have made the upstairs hospitable for my visit, but I'm afraid my generator seems to have given up under the snow. Is there a reason for your visit, Deputy? An emergency?"

"The snow." Bobby replied, repeating the

man's own words, caught in his gaze and lulled by the familiarly melodic intonation of his voice. Bobby could feel his heart racing and his skin prickling with sweat as he realised in that moment that James' guess was correct.

Bobby had no doubt Frederick — Rick — Reitz had taken the children.

Bobby's fingers twitched over his sidearm, and Reitz's gaze darted towards the movement and then back to Bobby's eyes, with a further curl to his smile.

"The Sheriff sending out deputies to check on the locals? It's very kind and thoughtful, I didn't realise anyone other than James knew I was visiting." The comment was so polite and casual that it was clear he wasn't threatened in the least by Bobby.

"James is..." Bobby's mouth was dry as he tried to say the words. "He passed."

The words brought with them a flood of emotion that felt like it might burst through at any moment. Had it only been a few hours? A day? It felt like time had stopped moving as it should as soon as the snow started. It felt that way every year, but now especially. With James gone, it felt like Elk Pass slipped a little further from the grips of reality.

"I'm sorry—" Reitz stepped forward as though he was going to reach out to comfort Bobby.

At that Bobby stepped back, hand ready on his gun.

"That's close enough."

Reitz's gentle smile was unnerving, and Bobby felt a tremor of something go through him, felt words trying to break through his thoughts. Because as much as he knew he should just continue on his journey out to Allen, there was something else bubbling up inside him. A confrontation he'd been waiting to have for twenty years.

"You left me behind." Bobby blurted out; the words full of more anger than he had ever realised he held. Thoughts of his shitty childhood with his alcoholic father, being sick all the time from neglect, and then missing that chance for a new life, whatever it held.

Reitz's features softened and he looked in that moment beautiful and terrifying, as though Bobby could see the man's true self. It was dark. A shadow. A beast.

It sent a thrill through Bobby.

He felt like he was regaining something that had been lost to him. Something that had been intended for him. Something that he had dreamt of almost every night for twenty years.

Twenty years since that night when a little ball of darkness within him had stirred.

"Yes, I can only apologise for that, Bobby. However, I cannot regret it." Reitz's smooth tone was an echo of the music he had drawn the children away with. The sound that Bobby had wanted to follow. Would have followed into damnation.

"You left me behind." Bobby growled the words again, his lip curling with anger. It took him a moment to realise he had unholstered his weapon and his hand now rose of its own volition. Levelling the gun at Reitz as though some part of him was desperate to protect himself from the shadows he saw in the man. Even as the rest of him wanted to be consumed by them.

"Bobby…" His name came out on a sigh as Reitz moved closer, putting his hand gently over Bobby's and guiding it down until his weapon was safely holstered once more.

He felt like he was trapped in a daze. The touch of the man's warm flesh against his own made him all the more eager to be swallowed up by the shadow that had been inescapable twenty years ago. He had been waiting to be swallowed whole by it ever since and had never planned to resist.

"Will you let me show you why I don't regret it? I promise no harm will come to you. And if you are willing to listen, then no harm will come to the town either."

"It was you." Bobby muttered, as his consciousness retreated from the grips of the shadow.

Yes, he had wanted to go, but this man had stolen the children and done who knows what with them. Bobby couldn't pretend to understand any of it. Only that, with James gone, he was the only person that stood between the townspeople of Elk Pass and the strange evil that haunted the place. The evil inside this man.

"Will you let me explain? Will you let me take you there?" Reitz was close now, Bobby could feel the heat of him, the scent of the woods lingering on his hair and clothes. He felt light-headed and dizzy when Reitz spoke.

Bobby felt as though Rick's thoughts made their way into his mind. He felt he was losing Bobby and he couldn't have that, he wanted to swallow him into the shadow.

The music in Reitz's voice took him back to his childhood, to that desire. The need to follow him.

Bobby already knew, no matter where it took him, he had to follow this time; he didn't want to fight it.

The snow was falling thickly, and he vaguely heard Buck whine as they walked past his truck. Bobby carried on, following the shadow man as he had all those years ago.

They walked into the treeline and, despite

how hazy his thoughts were becoming, Bobby expected that they would simply walk into a dense thicket.

But when they hit the edge of the woods — everything changed.

Bobby felt sick, like he was flipped over and over while standing still. He felt foggy. A few more steps in and he felt as though he was walking through a wall of jello.

And then, quite suddenly, he came out the other side.

The air seemed different and, while his disorientation was clearing, he felt sick to his stomach. He doubled over and vomited, a thick black substance that he was sure couldn't have come from his body.

Bobby straightened up, trembling all over as his mind grew clearer and the fogginess was relegated to his physical surroundings, only a hint of it hovering over his mind.

There was no snow, instead a stuffy sort of humidity surrounded him. The air was still, and the woods were lit with a warm orange glow that had no discernible source. Blossom filled the air, drifting in slow motion rather than falling, and seemingly never hitting the ground.

He felt comforted by the heat.

It reminded him of the vacation they had taken to visit his grandfather in Louisiana the summer before his mother left. It had been so warm, a constant heat he had never known having grown up in Elk Pass — a town that felt almost constantly stuck in winter.

But more than that, the memory had become more beautiful and comforting to him as the years had passed. As his sweaters became threadbare and the holes in his socks mattered little, considering the holes in his shoes — he wished for that warmth. His one good coat had been a size too small. The overwhelming feeling of his childhood was the bone chilling cold that seemed to consume him inside and out. All except that one bright time with his grandfather.

He had considered running away, trying to find that warm place again. Maybe his mother would be there? But then the children had disappeared, and he felt compelled to stay. Even when he grew to an age when he might take off on his own.

He had tried once. When he was seventeen, he had planned to catch a bus to the nearest city and then to who knew where. He made it two nights in the city before coming home. James and Mary had been so pleased to see him that they had never questioned why Bobby had gone and why he had returned.

And Bobby wouldn't readily tell anyone the truth of it. That the further he went from Elk Pass the more the memory of that music faded. He did not dream of the shadow man, and Bobby found he couldn't bear to live without it.

The thought of that now angered him.

"You kept me here." He muttered angrily as they walked. "I could have left, I wanted to leave, but you kept me here... waiting."

Reitz's smile was a little crooked, amused.

"*You* kept you here, Bobby. You could have left it all behind at any time. You could have made a new life somewhere else, the memories of this place and that night tucked away until you forgot them forever."

Bobby's cheeks burned, with rage or embarrassment he wasn't sure, either seemed a valid reaction to this truth.

"I'm sorry for any pain that I caused you." Reitz replied gently, the lyrical tone soothing Bobby for a brief moment before reigniting his anger.

"You're not sorry, one damn bit." He spat the words and stopped. "I just want to know... Why?"

Reitz turned to face him, his expression soft and a little unsure.

"Happy fortune? And a long story. But in the end, it comes down to one thing I suppose."

"And what's that?" Bobby snarled.

"Companionship." Reitz swept his hand in front of them in a flourish, indicating the path ahead before starting forward. Bobby couldn't help but follow him as he had twenty years earlier.

"They are all safe of course, I could never harm them. Not after... I could never hurt a child."

"Just their parents. Just the town," Bobby replied with venom in his voice.

"The same people who hurt me, hurt my family. Didn't protect us, didn't give us justice. And were happy to take any consequences rather than give me justice when they promised it. I warned them there would be consequences." Reitz bit back as he tread softly and silently through the woods.

Bobby had nothing to say to that. In his mind — *succulent* — echoed.

"So, they live here?" Bobby asked. *Wherever here is.*

"Yes. They are all my wards. But time moves differently here, they have hardly aged in these many years. They make for diverting company, but not as fulfilling as adults. Though you would be surprised at how intelligent and precocious children can be." He stopped and turned to look at Bobby, his eyes sweeping over him. "I crave the company of an adult, and the opportunity fate presented in you—"

"Fate!" Bobby snorted.

"Yes, fate." Reitz started to walk again, "I'd call it fate. That you were too sick to keep up, made sick by the neglect of your father and the abandonment of your mother. A woman whose lineage takes her back to Europe and—"

"How did you know that? What do you know about her?" Bobby snapped.

"Most white Americans are descended from Europeans; it could be a lucky guess if you'd prefer." Reitz dismissed.

"But it isn't."

"No, it isn't. I made it my business to know more of you, Bobby. I had a sense of you but needed to know more. And what I discovered was very interesting indeed. Perhaps you might be intrigued by my own past and where—"

"I don't give a shit about you," Bobby cut him off, hoping he didn't hear the lie in it. "I just care about whether the kids are safe."

Bobby clenched his jaw, stopping the words on the tip of his tongue. That he did want to know more. That he was deeply intrigued by the man, or the beast, who had left him behind.

Reitz gave an amused huff.

"Maybe later then," Frederick replied as they reached the end of the path through the dense treeline.

They broke through it as they had on the way in, though this time there was no gelatinous barrier. The woods were gone. Instead, there stood the town of Elk Pass, bathed in a setting, invisible sun and full of the sound of children laughing as they played in the blossom filled streets.

Despite the warmth, Bobby felt chilled by memories of his own lonely childhood where such sounds were absent after the night Reitz took them. He had known these children. They had aged so little, almost exactly the children he had gone to school with, bullies and acquaintances alike. As they went about their business, they looked at him and smiled, welcoming.

"They don't seem bothered to see another adult," Bobby observed.

"I have told them many times to expect you," Reitz replied, his voice a low and gentle rumble and his smile fond.

❦

Reitz walked him through the town in the weird half-light that was like no time of day or year that was familiar to Bobby. They had arrived at the Sheriff's office, or at least this version of the office, a dream version. A replica seen through a slightly unfocused lens. The office itself was musty and disused, as most things in this inside out town seemed to be, after all, what need did they have for it? The few residents here were all under the age of thirteen.

Even so, nothing looked to be decaying or showing signs of age and wear as they would in the real world. At most, some of the papers scattered on the desks were a little yellowed at the corners, and Bobby had to wonder if those had been brought from the real world.

The wall usually used for active investigation information was densely packed with all kinds of evidence and photographs. Family photos, birth certificates, the Reitz family tree. And alongside that, all kinds of information on Randall Allen.

Bobby stepped up to take a closer look.

There was one newspaper clipping, a report on the Allen heir's clear insanity and rumours of his involvement in the mysterious murder of the Reitz family.

"The one glint of truth."

Frederick stood a short distance off, near the door, lingering as though he hesitated to come in.

Bobby looked back to the article, such as it was, as Reitz continued: "You know, their murders were barely reported on at all, so well was it all covered up. Just that one piece of sensationalism that didn't even make the front page of a tabloid rag."

There was no emotion there. It was something the man had come to terms with perhaps. Or at least it was no longer so raw that he couldn't be objective.

After all, it had been more than thirty years.

Bobby shook his head. "It shouldn't have happened, he shouldn't have got away with it."

Reitz raised a brow.

"How much do you know?"

"You brought me here to get justice?" Bobby answered with his own question.

Reitz shook his head, "I brought you to this place because you belong here. I brought you to this office to... I want you to understand why I did what I did."

"Punishment. Vengeance." Bobby replied, looking at Reitz again and feeling the pull of frustration over his own undeniable connection to the man.

Perhaps their fates were tied together from the moment Elk Pass had let Randall Allen get away with his crimes.

"I know enough," Bobby continued when Reitz didn't respond. "I... James left me a note and pointed me in this direction. He was always terrified you would come back for me. And even more terrified that Allen would strike again."

"And now I have returned." Again that flat, emotionless tone. "The town did not deserve to keep any of its children, but I cannot regret that you were left behind. I know you can feel it too."

At that there was a slight quirk of his brow and an even slighter quirk of his lips.

"What is it you believe I feel?" Bobby asked, reminded of those family tales of a sixth sense of sight beyond vision. Was he to believe that Reitz had similar stories in his family?

"A connection. A kinship. Power." Reitz said the words with conviction. "I can see you as much as you can see me, Bobby. You were never meant to come with me then, because you are meant to be here now."

Bobby scoffed, huffing out a half laugh.

"You don't mean to help get justice, do you? What do you think is going to happen here? The town — *my town* — is about to be cut off for the winter. The Sheriff is dead and if dispatch was correct, we're about to be overrun with some sort of rodent infestation. You think I will stay here with you? Even if..." he hesitated over the words, because it wasn't an *if*, he did feel a connection and could sense that their capacity — the line they drew — was the same. They had the same shadow beast within them, Reitz had mastered his.

"Even if I felt a *connection*, why would I stay here when I am needed in Elk Pass?"

Reitz sighed gently.

"Bobby, if you let me explain, I will end the infestation. I will return the children to the town, to the jubilation of the residents. Giving them something to ease the pain of their beloved Sheriff's passing. I just ask one thing in return... and then you may leave me if you so wish. But I dearly hope you'll stay."

Bobby studied the man, he seemed resolute. And Bobby could not doubt his words, even in part, because what other option did he have? The last time the infestation ended with the loss of the children. What more could the town possibly lose?

"What's the catch?"

There was a moment of silence between them, during which Bobby realised that he had already made up his mind to agree to whatever it was. Whatever got these children finally home. Whatever saved the town from the slow death it had been experiencing for the last twenty years, with or without the infestation. If Reitz wanted him to stay here? So be it. James was gone, Mary had others to care for her. Buck would be happened upon and adopted. His whole life he had lived in that town and yet never had he grown substantial roots.

Never had he once presumed he would be missed.

If it was an exchange, so be it.

"I want you to help me kill Randall Allen."

Bobby woke in a cold sweat, panting and scrambling at the blanket covering him as he tried to come back to his senses. Tried to remember where he was and how he got there. This wasn't his usual nightmare of loneliness and abandonment, of darkness curling around him but never consuming him.

Instead, it was like his mind was clouded and numbed. The memories returned to him slowly. Foggy, as though waking from a dream in reverse. Waking into a dream.

The blanket fell away as Bobby sat and looked around, realising that he was sitting in his chair in the Sheriff's office. But not *his* chair, not *his* office. A facsimile of his office. He pulled the blanket back up to his lap, wondering when that had been placed on him. The dream-like memories came through the fog. The lack of sleep must have crept up on him.

They had talked for what felt like hours.

Bobby never outright said no to killing Allen, instead, despite the rising desire in him to kill the man, he had simply answered that he would help bring about justice.

That seemed to satisfy Reitz, who then took a seat beside him, and their conversation had begun in earnest. Bobby had asked questions about this place, about the children and their wellbeing, only to discover that it was Reitz's prime concern and consideration. Bobby found himself retelling memories he had of some of the children when he had known them years earlier. The conversation had naturally side-tracked here and there, and, surprisingly, Bobby found himself laughing with Reitz, talking with ease and enjoyment. Bobby had never before in his life been subject to this intent attention and found it strange at first. Not least because of the time and place, but because of the ease of it.

In a different time, had life been different, he and Frederick Reitz might have been friends. The thought brought an unexpected sensation to Bobby's gut and a blush to his cheeks.

He remembered the first few weeks of knowing James and Mary and them practically having to pry any information from him. But this had been easy. Enjoyable. Bobby had almost forgotten the gravity of the situation they found themselves in.

Slowly, as they spoke, he felt the vicious coil of resentment that had settled deep within his bones for over two decades, unwind. He felt this crackle of a connection between them dissipate the bitterness that he had held for Reitz, for the shadow man, for being left behind. He was finding, as the minutes and hours passed, that he was grateful.

He had never made a connection like this before, he had never so naturally made a friend, for he was sure that was what this was. And he couldn't be bitter about it. He couldn't resent having had to wait twenty years in order to have this connection. He found the bitterness slip from him to be replaced with a warmth at being able to now experience this as an adult, with the years of hurt and life behind him.

As Reitz had said, perhaps it *was* fate.

"Bobby, you're awake." Reitz was standing at the office door with a disarming smile and something steaming in a mug.

Bobby could only nod at the obvious and return the smile without thought.

"You nodded off."

Bobby nodded again, in acknowledgement. As much as he remembered enjoying their conversations, now things seemed even foggier. Even those discussions before he fell asleep felt almost surreal.

"Sure. How long have I been asleep?"

"Barely any time, maybe thirty minutes. Just long enough to recharge." Still that smile.

"Why... why are you smiling?" Bobby huffed his amusement. He was often blunt, but this haze descending around them was making it hard to filter himself. It wasn't unpleasant, but it felt like something seeping into him, like a drug, stripping him of some aspect of himself. Of the armour he'd built up over decades of loneliness.

"Can I be honest?" Reitz asked, a little sheepishly, setting down the mug and resuming a seat opposite Bobby.

Bobby raised a brow, waiting for Reitz to continue.

"I enjoy your company even more than I had anticipated." Reitz muttered and then cleared his throat. "I'm sorry, I know this must all seem so strange to you."

Bobby shook his head. "Strangely not as much as I'd have thought, but I feel you have more to do with that than you're letting on."

Reitz's jaw tightened but he ignored the remark and continued.

"I want to impress on you how sorry I am that I left you behind. I know that it has been hard for you, but I hope you can see now that it *was* necessary."

Bobby mulled this over. Now he was of an age and in a position to be of use to the man in his quest for justice or vengeance. He was of far more use now than he ever could have been as a child.

Bobby shrugged.

"You didn't leave me; I couldn't keep up." He said, though he had always felt abandoned, he knew that it was just as much the fault of his dad for his poor health stopping him. He felt almost at peace with it for the first time in his life.

Reitz's smile faltered. "That isn't strictly true. I could have waited for you to catch up. I could have stopped and carried you. But I didn't."

Bobby felt a sudden pain in his chest that he hadn't felt since the day his mother had left. A different kind of ache, now that he knew he truly had been abandoned. It felt doubly like a betrayal after the hours they had passed together. He had spent so many years trying not to think that and now to hear the truth of it was overwhelming.

"If you give me a chance to explain." Reitz continued cautiously, eyes clearly searching Bobby's for any outward sign of emotion, but he had set the armour back in place as much as was possible in this dream state. "Had it been merely a desire for an adult I could use to my own ends in my quest for justice against the Allens, I could have left any of the children. I could, quite possibly, have even recruited an adult back then. There were several who would have been glad to assist in any manner of pains visited upon the Allen family. Especially if there was a child to be bargained for."

"Then why?" Bobby asked, trying to keep the pain from his tone.

"I sensed something in you, Bobby. It was very clear to me immediately that you were special, you were like me. I knew then that I had to wait, and not just for an adult accomplice. For a… for a partner, a companion. There is more, it's difficult to explain..."

"I could never do what you did. Steal the children—"

"No?" Reitz asked, his tone challenging and teasing. "We all react differently than we might presume when under unexpected stressors."

"I thought you worked with wildlife. You

sound like a therapist." Bobby huffed angrily.

"I am. That is my profession in the waking world. I study the minds of humans, the most prevalent species on the planet." He stopped, almost as though expecting and waiting for the snort that Bobby then gave, before he continued. "I have tried in my own way to make sense of my reaction to the death and mutilation of my family. It was my uncle who helped me finally understand it all. Those ten years away from here were not idly spent. I planned this, should I not get the justice my family deserved. I…" He looked meaningfully at Bobby. "I did not plan *you*. It was a surprise to find one such as yourself amongst the children, and I knew immediately you were meant for other things. I couldn't take you, couldn't leave you in this place."

"This is all just double talk. You're saying you left me so that I could grow up, but I still don't understand why and what role you see me having in all of this. I'm an officer of the law. I'm," Bobby took in a breath and released it slowly. "I'm not going to help you kill Randall Allen."

Bobby tried to hold the conviction of his words.

Reitz nodded his understanding. "And I will accept that if you so choose. But first… I, Bobby, I want to talk about your mother."

Taken aback, Bobby held back an angry retort, instead spitting out, "you truly are a therapist!"

Reitz let out a low chuckle at that but pressed on.

"Let me explain what I know. When you caught my attention and I left you behind I looked into your family, your history. Your mother's family originally came from a small town in Northern Europe. In the Netherlands to be exact. Not so very far from where my family originated. Close enough that the connection was then obvious to me. You and I, Bobby, my family, your mother… we aren't wholly in this world. It is the only reason you can be here and not lose yourself to the daze of it as the children have. I know it is beginning to wear on you now as you have not fully become yourself, but on the whole you would remain unaffected. Imagine how these years would have felt to you if you had experienced them all in your mind but remained bodily a child? I did not want that for you."

"I don't understand…" Bobby almost whimpered. His mind was full of information that seemed to thread through him and end loosely, waiting to come together.

"The humans in my birth country call us *die feen*. Fae."

"Fairies?" Bobby nearly barked a laugh, but the look on Reitz's face stifled it.

"Some call us monsters or demons." Reitz continued, darkly. "Humans have lots of words for things they don't understand."

Reitz took a breath before continuing gently, "your mother left because she met someone else."

"No." Bobby said firmly, though he knew from his dad's litany of curses that it was true. He just never wanted to believe that she left *him*, left him there with his dad for someone else.

"She died." Bobby said firmly. This was also true, though he only found out years later when he began looking into it himself. She had re-located to Ontario when she had left, it seemed a world away even now as an adult. She had been killed in a car crash a few months later. An accident, someone not paying attention, brakes not gripping quickly enough. That was that. That was why she never came back for him. Discovering it had eased one pain and struck another.

As if reading his mind, Reitz spoke in a soothing tone.

"She would have come back for you. It is hard for those like us to be without kin, a difficult and lonely existence that your mother surely felt keenly. She met another like her, with fae blood. He died also. But they would have come back for you once they were settled. They may not have even known what that attraction was between them, the call of their blood drew them together."

Bobby was shaking. Rage and agony roiled around inside him, threatening to burst forth.

No matter what he wanted to believe about his mother, he knew the truth and… what Reitz had said, he somehow knew that was true as well.

When Reitz leaned forward and took his hands, Bobby didn't protest. In fact, the contact sent a vibration through him, like a circuit being completed.

"You tried to make a home here, tried to find comfort in the Sheriff and his wife, but… you should be with your own people. Whether me or another but… I would prefer you to be with me. I… have been lonely, too."

Bobby realised he was trembling as he felt emotion flowing between their touching bodies. All these years he had thought of Frederick Reitz, one way or another. That shadow beast that had taken the children. Cursed him for the abandonment, wondered what it might have been like to go wherever the other children had, even if it had been to their deaths.

And now he knew Reitz had spent those years thinking of him too. Waiting. Not just for an accomplice but for something *more*. Kinship. Not to be alone.

"I don't know what you're asking of me,"

Bobby murmured. "It isn't just to help kill Allen, is it?"

"It can be. Or more than that. The choice is yours. I can take you back to Elk Pass now and never bother you again. But I hoped... Allen or not, I hoped that you would come with me, back to the old country. It's... it's different there, Bobby. *You* will be different. Your power will be stronger. You have a sense inherited from your mother, but that is just the tip of it. You could be deadly; you could be benevolent. You're shot through with the light that runs within all fae and is dimmed so much here. You will become what you were always meant to be."

Bobby let out a breath he didn't realise he had been holding. He shuddered when Reitz's thumbs stroked across the back of his hands.

"I will kill Randall Allen; I will have justice for my family. I cannot deny that I have a strong desire for you to help me, for you to embrace that dark nature and power within you. To fully awaken the fae that you are. A people who could read the hearts of those around them and fight so fiercely as to slay dragons. If you choose not to, I hope that you still might consider learning more about our kind."

Bobby looked up at Reitz, not wanting to pull his hands away.

He had never felt as complete as in that moment, in that connection. The truth was clear even through the haze of this other world. In that moment he knew himself better than he ever had before. He knew that there was a shadow inside him that wanted to rise.

"The kids, they… do they know? Do they understand where they are?"

"As much as they can. I had aimed to keep this as painless as possible for them. To them it seems just a dream."

"I feel drugged. The longer I am here. I feel foggy and numb. Do they feel that way?"

Reitz nodded. "Yes, to a greater degree. A mild sedation in a sense. To them hardly any time has passed and certainly not enough for them to ask questions or be concerned."

"They're too stoned to ask questions." Bobby huffed, caught somewhere between unhappy at that thought and glad they were saved from the suffering of missing their families the way their families hadn't been spared.

"Perhaps," Reitz smiled and squeezed his hands. "Don't you think that is for the best? Would you have them fully aware and upset?" The smile slowly faded, and Reitz looked a little distant. "I could never hurt a child, Bobby. I could never see them harmed. They have all lived here safely, happily. In a dream. I would never punish them for their parents' lack of compassion for my sister's plight. As I said, bringing you here… this place doesn't affect you as it does them. You would have been aware, and I couldn't have done that to you, to any child."

Bobby's jaw tightened and he found he wanted to reach for Reitz and comfort him in some way, but he didn't. Few times in his life had he felt the urge to physically comfort someone else, mostly because there was no one that close to him. And now this practical stranger...

But he wasn't a stranger. This connection had started twenty years ago when Bobby had been spellbound by Frederick Reitz's music. When he had been unable to follow and felt bereft. Had to learn over the long and unhappy years of his childhood to deal with the pain of that abandonment and separation, one just as great as when his mother had left.

But on top of that, to never speak about it, never acknowledge it.

He *wanted* to acknowledge it.

A few moments of silence passed and then he found himself squeezing Reitz's hands in return.

"You did more than their parents deserved." Bobby told him, wanting to ease his pain and remembering Allen's tape, remembering James' notes.

"I wanted to save them, Bobby." The words trembled. "He is still there, still alive and free. I didn't want any other child to be his victim."

Bobby had thought that he had started to

understand Reitz, but it was as though the last veil had finally been lifted. He was a monster, that much was true, but his heart was filled with a love for his sister that stretched to all the children in his care.

"Yes, Frederick." Bobby answered the question he had been asked so long before. "Yes, I will help you kill Randall Allen."

Chapter Four

Frederick explained that beyond the central streets the town faded, his replica was not complete. Just enough to fool the children for whom so little time had passed. In this reality, where Bobby Taylor's house — his father's house — should stand, there was nothing. An emptiness. It seemed sort of fitting, considering the number of times he'd wanted to pull the place down.

Frederick led Bobby back to the woods and towards land that should belong to the Reitz House. And there, Frederick explained, was where he had thinned the wall between the worlds. Not a dream state, as it felt, but another world.

One only the fae could open.

The woods seemed to expand and contract around them now that Bobby felt more aware of the effect. When they passed through this time, he didn't feel sick or ill-adjusted. It felt as though his body was now attuned to the shift in reality.

Back in the real world the snow had stopped but the sky was so clouded with grey it was hard to know the time of day. Layers of the thick snow crunched beneath their feet, and they had to avoid several drifts. The shelter of the trees meant that it was less deep here, but Bobby knew that the town would be snowed in. He wondered whether the salting and ploughing had been put into action as it should have been, keeping clear the road and bridge out of town.

It seemed like such a distant concern, under the circumstances.

He wasn't sure how much time had passed by the time they were back at his truck. Buck was curled up asleep in the footwell with a blanket he'd pulled off the seat. It suddenly felt so strangely normal. Life. If his life had ever been normal.

The reverie lasted exactly as long as it had taken for him to look in and see Buck was safe. Then, in short order, he heard a strange rustling noise at the same time as his radio sparked back into life.

"Bobby, Bobby! Are you there, please, dammit!" He woke Buck as he opened the door to grab for the CB. Before he'd had a chance to answer Bryony's call, the rustling became a scrabbling. A cacophony of noise swarmed them, drowning out any further words Bryony desperately shouted down the line.

It took him a moment to realise that the sound he could hear on the other end of the radio wasn't just there, but beside him too. All around them.

Frederick did not seem at all phased as Bobby realised the ground was moving.

The snow was shifting and pulsating around

them, as if earth itself was trembling, until the cause became clear.

Large, plump rats hurtled past them. The snow was left a mess by thousands of tiny feet. They swarmed over Bobby and Frederick's boots, weaving in and out. It took minutes on end for the bulk of the rats to retreat — which was clearly what they were doing — leaving no little destruction in their wake.

Bobby turned to Frederick.

"You called them off?"

He no longer had any doubt in his mind about the connection between the infestation twenty years earlier and Frederick. It had been a simple thing really, a hustle. Resolve something you caused in return for what you want. A manipulation, but one that would have been necessary in order to pursue justice, and even then, it didn't work.

"Called them off? Not exactly. They only have one target now. They will lead us to Randall Allen."

Bobby nodded and got into his vehicle, inviting Frederick to do the same. They waited for the stream of rats to thin before he started to drive slowly after them, trying not to run any of them over as they scrabbled at a speed he couldn't fathom.

They devastated everything in their path, blazing a trail to the Allen Estate, relative neighbours of the Reitz.

"I didn't think Randall Allen lived here any-more?" Bobby commented.

"Perhaps visiting?" Frederick responded as they pulled up the drive to find a very expensive car haphazardly parked, the driver's door open. Some of the rats swarmed into it and began destroying the interior.

Bobby didn't need years as a deputy to tell him that something was very amiss at this place, regardless of the current circumstance of the heavy snowfall and a rampaging horde of rats. He drew his sidearm as they approached the house carefully, trying to avoid the rats that still moved in waves across the snow.

"I want you to be the one to kill him," Frederick commented, nodding at Bobby's sidearm. "But not like that."

Bobby stilled, surprised at the outright confession but didn't lower his weapon. Frederick's determined look sent a tremor through him, one he tried to ignore as he continued on. When they reached the steps up to the house the sight before them pulled his focus entirely.

The front door was wide open, a small snow drift built up just inside the threshold and ensured that it wouldn't close without some effort. The rats went no further than the snow, surging up to but not through the door itself as though caught on a tide.

Bobby realised that the door wasn't just open but hanging strangely. It was a large door, but it had been forced and now the hinges were threatening to give out. A forced entry. That was all he needed to know in order to act.

He flicked off the safety on his gun and was prepared to cock it, ready for anything.

He hoped.

Anything seemed so broad now, broad enough to encompass unageing children living in a secret fae pocket reality.

Bobby carried on cautiously into the house, not calling out for the residents, ever alert. He could feel Frederick behind him, though the man seemed to move with much less caution.

They were nearing the end of the large and ornately decorated foyer when they heard it.

Bobby was almost completely certain that it wasn't the blood curdling scream that made Frederick stride past him, but the maniacal laughter that followed it.

Frederick, now in the lead, raced towards the back of the house, following the laughter down a dark hallway. He moved quickly through the oppressive space towards the dim light at the end of it. Bobby followed while trying to remain as alert as possible and wondering whether or not he should tell Frederick to get back behind him. The man was unarmed, and they had no idea what they were walking into, but equally —

Frederick was clearly able to handle himself. The fae power he held surged off of him.

The hallway soon gave way to a kitchen and the scene before them was a desperate one.

Randall Allen, who appeared to be in his pyjamas and a smoking jacket, stood at the far side of the room with a dark-haired woman in his grasp. He had her held tight around the waist and had a knife pressed to her throat, a small line of blood already erupting through the skin.

"Randall, I swear..." another woman, older and surely Dawn Allen, stood on the other side of a breakfast bar.

"Now, now, Dawn. Look, we have guests, and you know father would never have approved of you keeping your whore here with you. In *his* house, Dawn!" There was a mock indignation there and he didn't miss a beat as his eyes flicked between Bobby and Frederick as they entered the room.

Bobby kept his gun levelled, aimed squarely at the man and his human shield.

"Let the woman go, Allen."

Bobby had not been sure what to expect upon meeting the man, but this situation had pushed him quickly back into deputy mode and he was reminded of having to kill Robson.

He'd *had* to do that then. He had to do this now.

His request was met with more maniacal laughter.

"Driven from my own home? I came back here to stake my claim and found these bitches trying to besmirch our family name with their disgusting ways."

"He's mad. He's fucking insane!" Dawn raged, a hint of terror along with the anger.

Randall Allen sneered at her and lowered the knife from the woman's throat to her belly.

"Don't think I don't know about this, Dawn! Trying to replace our little family? What would father say?" The words were spat angrily before he switched back again to a tone Bobby could only call deeply crazy. "He'd say you should have been born with a penis!" Randall let out a burst of crazed laughter.

"Shoulda, coulda, woulda. Who made this one for you, hmm? Some filthy homosexual friend? Did you let him fuck her Dawn? Did dear Elaine get to feel the touch of a man? I bet she loved it. I'd have fucked her if you'd asked, held her down and made her feel a real Allen, put a real Allen inside her." He grinned sickeningly and licked his tongue flatly up the side of the woman's face.

Elaine's expression wavered from resilience to terror.

If he'd had a clean shot then, Bobby would have taken it.

He saw Dawn's knuckles grow white as she clutched at the bench. She was biting her tongue with eyes completely focused on the knife that Randall was now swirling gently over the woman's barely rounded belly.

There seemed to be a stillness in the air.

No one wanted to cause a ripple that might result in devastation.

After a few moments Frederick stepped forward, moving around Bobby and Dawn and towards Randall who seemed too surprised and amused to act.

"Now Randall, this is quite unnecessary. Let your sister and her friend leave and we will discuss this situation like adults."

Randall barked another laugh at that, but clearly, he recognised Frederick.

"I knew it was you. These rodents, just like last time. People thought *I* was mad, I told them it was you back then and they didn't believe me!"

"You appear to be correct," Frederick smiled gently, as though talking to a child. "Why your response to my presence has been to come here, I don't know, but we should talk, without the ladies present."

Randall looked like he was considering this in earnest for a moment but then spat back angrily, "I'm here because this is my home. This is where I belong. If you're going to come and try to take me, like you took the children, then you are mistaken. I am staying here. You can take these bitches instead. Take Dawn if it's an Allen you want. Or this little one if it's children you want."

He pressed the knife to Elaine's belly, and she let out a strangled sob.

Bobby noticed Dawn flinch and she looked as though she were about to move forward, a knee-jerk reaction. But she stopped, and from her expression Bobby couldn't tell if she was holding herself back, or if she was being held back by something else.

He looked to Frederick, whose expression was still calm, collected.

Randall began to rant nonsensically about reclaiming his birthright. Perhaps he hoped his father would rise from the dead to protect him again. Given the last couple of days, Bobby wondered whether that might actually happen. And still had absolute faith that Frederick would triumph in whatever was coming next.

Randall continued to babble, his words meaning nothing and a mixture of rage and fear threading through his tone as his eyes remained fixed on Frederick.

Finally, he said something that made sense, and sent a chill running through Bobby.

"If it's revenge you want then take it." The man screamed. "Take Dawn, she's as sweet as a peach. *Succulent*." His face cracked into a wide grin.

Frederick's reaction was so fast that Bobby

barely registered it. He went from standing beyond arm's length to in front of Randall in the blink of an eye, taking the hand that held the knife and snapping it back with such force that the sound of bones breaking echoed around the room.

Elaine let out a sob as she used the opportunity to escape his grasp. She damn near fell into Bobby's arms. He holstered his gun and held her up, shuffling her over to Dawn who immediately took hold of the woman.

Frederick still had Randall's arm twisted in his hand, Randall sank to his knees under the pain of it. His scream was silent, his expression torn between anger and terror. When he finally regained his trembling voice, he spat and swore obscenities and curses at them — the outburst of a scalded child that went ignored by them all.

"Ms Allen, many years ago your father protected your brother from paying for a crime. I do not think you are a stranger to his abuses. So perhaps I don't need to ask this. Are you going to side with your father here and protect him, or can we presume that you are happy for him to finally pay for his crimes? All of his crimes."

Frederick's words weren't cold, but his eyes were, and Dawn met them with a stern gaze, holding her lover to her as she sneered, "do what you like with him, as long as it's painful, and as long as he ends up dead."

Randall poured forth a mixture of nervous laughter and raving pleas for mercy as Dawn helped her partner from the room without a backward glance.

"Daaa-wwn" Allen sing-songed her name as he tried to call her back. "You can't leave me! I won't let you!"

The door to the kitchen closed with a click that bounced off the walls.

Maybe the music had been playing quietly the whole time, but Bobby only really noticed it when the sound in the kitchen was reduced to just Randall's erratic and slightly menacing breathing. He could feel, rather than hear, that Frederick was the source. A melodic tune so familiar to him from his youth and his dreams, the lullaby used to lure the children through the snow. It vibrated off of the man.

Randall threw his hands over his ears once he registered it, and started near-screaming, "la la la, can't hear you!"

Frederick's grin was as disturbing as it was menacing. His eyes were dark and held a furious satisfaction, in that moment Frederick looked as deranged and consumed as Randall Allen. Bobby wondered if he should be terrified too.

Because one thing was clear, he was not needed here. Frederick had sought justice for his sister through the townsfolk and resorted to taking the children. Now he resorted to physical revenge, and it was oh so very clear, regardless of having asked, that he did not need any help from Bobby.

"Why am I here?" Bobby asked. His eyes on Randall's antics, though Frederick haunted his periphery, looming over Randall as the air around him started to swell and retract — like the barrier in the woods. It seemed that Randall was rooted to the spot whether he knew it or not, he danced from foot to foot but never out of a small area. That was the music, Bobby knew, he could feel that from Frederick too. He now understood what it was to be fae, the power they could have and wield.

The lights flickered and went out with a bang that startled only Randall.

The dim glow through the large kitchen windows and patio door gave an eerie aspect to the space but little illumination. And yet it was enough to see the dark shadow cast across Frederick, distorting his form...

He stood taller, now a shadow as black as night, wearing a thicket crown.

So familiar to Bobby. He had seen him like this before. In dreams where he had been left behind, abandoned by that retreating figure leading the children away. Frederick's true self.

Bobby had seen it that night.

"You don't need my help." Bobby shouted over the music, as Frederick's form wavered between the two and the light ebbed and waned with the movement of clouds and the snowstorm outside.

"No," the expression was soft, and it should have seemed strange on such a face but wasn't. Not to Bobby. "If I was to return for you Bobby, no matter whether you believed a word I said, I knew you would believe in your own lineage."

Never fear what you might become, sweetheart.

Bobby shivered as his mother's words echoed in his head. Had she known? Had she instinctively understood something of their nature?

"What do you want?" Bobby wondered aloud and turned his entire focus on Frederick, his subtly shifting form.

"Your true self," Frederick said gently, voice cutting through the music.

Randall continued to hop about, but it was no distraction, almost like he wasn't there at all behind a wall of music that was growing louder and louder.

"A killer?" Bobby asked, remembering Robson, remembering how that had felt. Powerful, alive. Righteous and victorious.

"Gods have power over life and death, one way or another," Frederick's voice was deeper, richer and darker than it had been.

"Are you saying the Fae are Gods, Frederick?" Bobby challenged.

"Our blood is holy." Frederick's words were almost dismissive.

"So, we are... created in God's image." Bobby agreed then.

"It is our right to bring life or death as we see fit and just." Frederick encouraged.

Bobby hummed his understanding, watching enjoyment burst across Frederick's face as Randall looked on the verge of dancing himself to death.

"We have that power." Frederick's voice was a rumble within his melody.

The music stopped abruptly. His face was cold and stern as Randall stopped, too, dropping to the floor, exhausted.

With the music gone Bobby could hear him again now, panting and sobbing.

"So... I have to kill Randall." Bobby stated and found a sort of truth in it, already knowing there was more to it. "Because you want me to embrace my nature."

"He deserves to die." Frederick replied.

Bobby couldn't disagree. He'd killed Robson for less, it felt. He looked down at Randall, who was sobbing and laughing and seemed now a pitiful, squirming creature. Bobby wondered how no one had killed him before. Well, now that Mayor Allen was gone...

"It's about power." Bobby said.

"It's about realising that power." Frederick spoke in a way that made clear he had no doubt that Bobby would help kill Randall as they had agreed, regardless. "You have been stuck in this Elk Pass, Bobby. You have adapted to this environment instead of the one meant for us. There is an evil in this place that perhaps drew my family, drew yours. An evil that many might think was me, the beast that took the children. But it goes deeper than that, it's a human evil, and it ends tonight. With the end of this Allen line."

At that the air around them stilled, and it was like that dream place again — the air thick and hanging with dust, like blossom floating on water. It made Bobby a little dizzy.

"You must become the creature you were always meant to be. And taking this life, setting right the evil that has plagued this place... you will come into the power that was always intended for you."

"And if I don't..." Bobby mused aloud, "I can't be with you."

"When I go, where I go, it is like this. It will affect you poorly should you not embrace what your blood insists you must."

Bobby felt his chest ache. A realisation he had already come to. He wanted to go with Frederick. He always had. For twenty years he had.

And this was the price he had to pay.

A small one, really.

Frederick grabbed Randall by the scruff and pulled him bodily from the floor. Randall let out a squeal of terror but seemed unable to move on his own in this thick haze.

"Do you know how the Allens made their fortune, Bobby? They were pig farmers. For generations they reared and slaughtered pigs, their money made them important in this town. Wealth bought them status and position. They became powerful the way evil men do. But at the end of the day, they are merely pig farmers," Frederick reached into his pocket with a sneer, seemingly repulsed by the knife he had pocketed from Randall before.

It looked old and well-used.

"Yours, yes?" He asked Randall as he pulled the knife free and opened it in one hand. The other still holding fast the whimpering man as he realised it to be the knife confiscated by police years earlier. The one he used to kill the Reitz family.

Bobby watched as he slowly slid the sharp blade into Randall's thigh. It went in as though easing into butter. The man's scream was stolen by the thick haze that surrounded them, as though he was underwater. Frederick's face betrayed no emotion and Bobby found himself saying, "this man butchered your family."

At that Frederick twisted the blade as he withdrew it, agony shooting through his expression while Randall nearly crumpled in on himself.

Bobby pulled his own hunting knife from his belt and moved forward until Randall was essentially pressed between them.

"They slice the throat of pigs, hang them to drain them. Slice their bellies and let the entrails fall out," Bobby mused dispassionately.

Frederick's lips tweaked into a small smile, and he raised Randall's knife to its owner's throat. The thickness dropped from the air then, reality resuming and Randall's screams loud and panicked filled the space around them along with the scent of urine.

Bobby could have been startled but wasn't. He pressed his own knife to Randall's belly, as Allen had done with the woman earlier.

"For Marlene." Frederick growled and drew the knife violently across Randall's throat. Bobby pulled back and plunged the knife through the layers of cloth, skin and fat, into the man's gut. Rending him.

Randall's mouth fell into a soundless scream as blood sprayed from his throat, washing over Bobby as the man's entrails fell at his feet.

"This is how man used to sacrifice to the Gods," Frederick bit out the words.

He released Randall and the man dropped lifeless to the floor into his own waste, blood and viscera still oozing from him.

There was an absolute silence.

The music was gone, the scurrying sound of rats was gone. Not even the sound of breathing in the room as they studied each other over Randall's body.

Bobby closed his eyes and brought it all back.

He could feel it.

The power.

His connection not just to Frederick but to everything, to life itself.

He opened his eyes and the air thickened; the haze returned with no ill-effect to him. He looked at Frederick and saw his crowned form, knowing that he himself reflected it. The music had resumed, but it wasn't the same. It was a lullaby his mother had sung him as a child. Bobby knew in that moment that it was his creation, the music was coming from him. He had that power.

He could see it all, he could feel it.

Surging around them both with little effort from him, just a gentle guide to this other world that he had always belonged to. The music seemed different than before. It felt like the truth. He understood it now.

"You've felt this power once before." Frederick told him, as though reading his mind. "But you didn't understand it then. You do now. You can harness it now."

Frederick was a man again as he stepped

towards Bobby and took his hand. Bobby was panting then, breathless at his own power, he let Frederick pull them close together. Blood pooled around their feet as they embraced.

"This is why I had to leave you before. But I won't leave you again," Frederick murmured against his cheek.

Bobby's heart swelled painfully in his chest, a sense of belonging and love that he had never felt before. He choked out a sob, overwhelmed.

He trembled, breathing heavily as he turned his head and found Frederick's lips with his own, tasting at first delight, then hesitation, and then surrender, set against the metallic taste of blood.

They had left Dawn Allen and Elaine Jackson standing outside the Allen Mansion, surrounded by the devastation of the rats, with instructions on where to find the children.

Frederick had lifted the veil of that place and now they would be found sleeping soundly in a warm clearing in the woods, having barely aged in the twenty years they had been gone.

Bobby had felt an obligation, that he should stay and help with the children. Help find those families that had moved away. But he knew he didn't belong in this place anymore, not now that he saw the world as Frederick did, the way he was always truly meant to.

Maybe it was a fair exchange? The one remaining child from that night for the return of all the others.

And it wasn't a hardship. Perhaps he might have hesitated a moment had James still been alive. He would have owed the man more than to simply vanish. But Mary would be fine without him, the Sheriff's Department would manage.

Though it was all moot, Bobby realised, as they drove from the town.

The snow was falling heavily again and within the hour the town was sure to be cut off for the rest of the winter. James had been right to be worried. The salt had not been laid and soon the bridge wouldn't be passable. The children would be found and cared for, the town would come together, and they would all cope, until the roads opened up again.

As they departed, Bobby had this strange sense, not so much a premonition but a sense of what was to come. He had always been able to feel things others couldn't, but this was more than that.

He could see clearly what lay ahead.

He could see Dawn Allen razing the Allen Estate to the ground, burning everything that was left of the Allen family legacy until all that remained was herself and the family she protected. He saw families reuniting, acting as a balm for the wound left by James' passing. He felt the darkness, which had always seemed to have a stranglehold on the town, start to lift.

As they cleared the bridge, Bobby looked in the rearview mirror as if for some confirmation. And perhaps the perpetual fog that seemed to always surround the town was gone. It looked brighter, and with all the snow, the town glistened. It felt like they had freed the place from an evil that had lived there, toxic and insidious.

Bobby looked over at Frederick in the passenger seat of his truck. Buck sat between them, tongue lolling as he took in the road ahead. Frederick looked so composed, as though completely unfazed by everything that had passed.

And while that seemed to be the case, Bobby could see through it. The composure, for once, was a ruse.

This man, this fae, was going to take him back to his roots, would teach him more about his true self.

This man — so powerful and self-assured. Bobby could see the cracks in him, light shining through the chinks in Frederick's armour, caused by his very existence. With Bobby he was the weakest man in the world, and Bobby already knew the same was true of himself.

He leaned over and took hold of Frederick's hand, drawing it across until Frederick had to shuffle along the seat, Buck now half across his lap, so that Bobby could rest their linked hands on his own thigh. Frederick laced their fingers together and Bobby looked across at him again.

He was smiling in a way that Bobby knew he hadn't since childhood.

And that made Bobby feel powerful.

ABOUT THE AUTHOR

Max Turner is a gay transgender man based in the United Kingdom. He writes speculative and science fiction, fantasy, horror, furry fiction and LGBTQ+ romance and erotica, and more often than not, combinations thereof.

You can find out more about Max and his work on his website: www.maxturneruk.com

THE CREDITS

Creating a book is a massive team effort.

Knight Errant and Max Turner would like to thank everyone who worked behind the scenes to make *The Child of Hameln* happen.

Managing Director and Editor

Nathaniel Kunitsky

Publishing Assistant

Friday Schoemaker

Creative Director

Lenka Murová

Project Assistant

Angelica Curzi

Cover Art Illustrator

Ares Bor

A special thank you to every single person who backed and shared our Kickstarter campaign.

Without your support our 2023 list would not have been possible.

m. turner j. hudson gabriella b. page e. morrison julie l. penland l. kraus e. bowers
o. whitney h. duncan e. claybaugh friday lindz e. reed andreas p. casey y. mittal k. sietel
brigh w. mamuna k. allen k. vikings c. page l. o'brien c. wair a. stanback b. hughes r. novak
c. cox p. kimble m. otto elena noel e. r. craig d. skea i. g. morris e. pitner dpn marina
d. psmith c. barron j. bottles i. birman j. thompson k. blair s. mayer a. penland f. rossero
dlhalp s. lloyd o. pinchuk h. mcdaid m. paley c. lewis k. lennon C r. rush-morgan vince
j. l. smith w. hughes n. hardy a. mcquaid eris anna caith zaraegis s. dunlop b. cebulski
syksy r. jones g. gregory f. ostby Creative Scotland c. donaldson j. cooper h. hirst
r. mccleary c. alexandersson sara r. vance a. jehangir daniil b. norton ophelia j. alexander
l. burwitz d. malcom k. hunziker j. oui k. turner d. carol alexandra sian gareth s. jones
fitakaleerie j. q. peterson karen rós k. CM r. page claire a. frank a. traphagan missy cara
PG m. piper a. treacy d. penland n. briggs ninedin a. grunwald p. carroll jake a. vaughn
morgan holly f. daoinsidhe c. post p. sterk Argonaut Books e. thompson sam
g. felker-martin kimberly m.p. deutsch t. orosz connie c. brienne s. mcphail g. bard
s. ingram e. van doren rxbin ian r. heafield p. stanton s. mckinlay r. rusak r. tonks j. bay
sophie d. b. moose patience n. williams c. withers áine s. cole harriet j. cole s. pybus dokja
m. noone isabela k. guilliams j. tövissy MW anna a. anderson tenille adam shana i. m. leigh
l. croal el s. smalley bethany idontfindyouthatinteresting m. huxley p. strömberg t. wymore
t. bridges c. luca l. bradley l. burns n. queen r. lindstrom p. herterich a. r. cardno p. reitz
g. casillas s. kollman b. weiss k. macaskill-smith s. norman c. j. gibson k. frey simon c.
e. davidson rayanroar n. novak midnightmare s. fraser c. spann tania c. morton j. cleak
rachlette m. young l. kapusta j. osborne k. lovick scarlet g. mitchell l. benson j. curtis
rachel owlglass i. sheene

OTHER WORK BY KNIGHT ERRANT PRESS

ABOUT
KNIGHT ERRANT PRESS

Knight Errant Press is a queer micro press based in Falkirk, Scotland, established in 2017.

We have a focus on LGBTQIA+ and inter-sectional storytelling and creators, and work within most genres and print formats.

Showcasing new and emerging writers' careers is our ambition, and we strive to find 2 or 3 works a year to bring to the world.

You can find out more about us at
www.knighterrantpress.com